Text © 2019 by Andrée Poulin
Illustrations © 2019 by Véronique Joffre
Translated by Karen Li

Published in English in 2019 by Owlkids Books Inc.

Published with the permission of Comme des géants inc.,
38, rue Sainte-Anne, Varennes
Québec, Canada J3X 1R5
All rights reserved.
Translation rights arranged through VeroK Agency, Spain.

Owlkids Books acknowledges the financial support of the Canada Council for the Arts, the
Ontario Arts Council, the Government of Canada through the Canada Book Fund (CBF) and
the Government of Ontario through the Ontario Media Development Corporation's Book
Initiative for our publishing activities.

Published in Canada by
Owlkids Books Inc.
1 Eglinton Avenue East
Toronto, ON M4P 3A1

Published in the United States by
Owlkids Books Inc.
1700 Fourth Street
Berkeley, CA 94710

Library and Archives Canada Cataloguing in Publication
Poulin, Andrée
[N'aie pas peur. English]
      When you're scared / written by Andrée Poulin ; illustrated by Véronique Joffre.
Translation of: N'aie pas peur.
ISBN 978-1-77147-365-1 (hardcover)
      I. Joffre, Véronique, 1982-, illustrator II. Title. III. Title: When you
are scared. IV. Title: N'aie pas peur. English.
PS8581.O837N3413 2019   jC843'.54   C2018-903435-1

Library of Congress Control Number: 2018946405

The text is set in Muli Light.

Manufactured in Dongguan, China, in October 2018,
by Toppan Leefung Packaging & Printing (Dongguan) Co., Ltd.
Job #BAYDC58

A   B   C   D   E   F

Publisher of Chirp, Chickadee and OWL | Owlkids Books is a division of Bayard CANADA
www.owlkidsbooks.com

When You're Scared

by ANDRÉE POULIN   illustrated by VÉRONIQUE JOFFRE

Owlkids Books

He's a little scared.

He's a little scared.

He's very scared.

He's very scared.

Grooouuu!

They're very scared.

Beep!
Beep!
Beeeep!

She's very scared.

He's very scared.

They're no longer scared.

They're no longer scared.

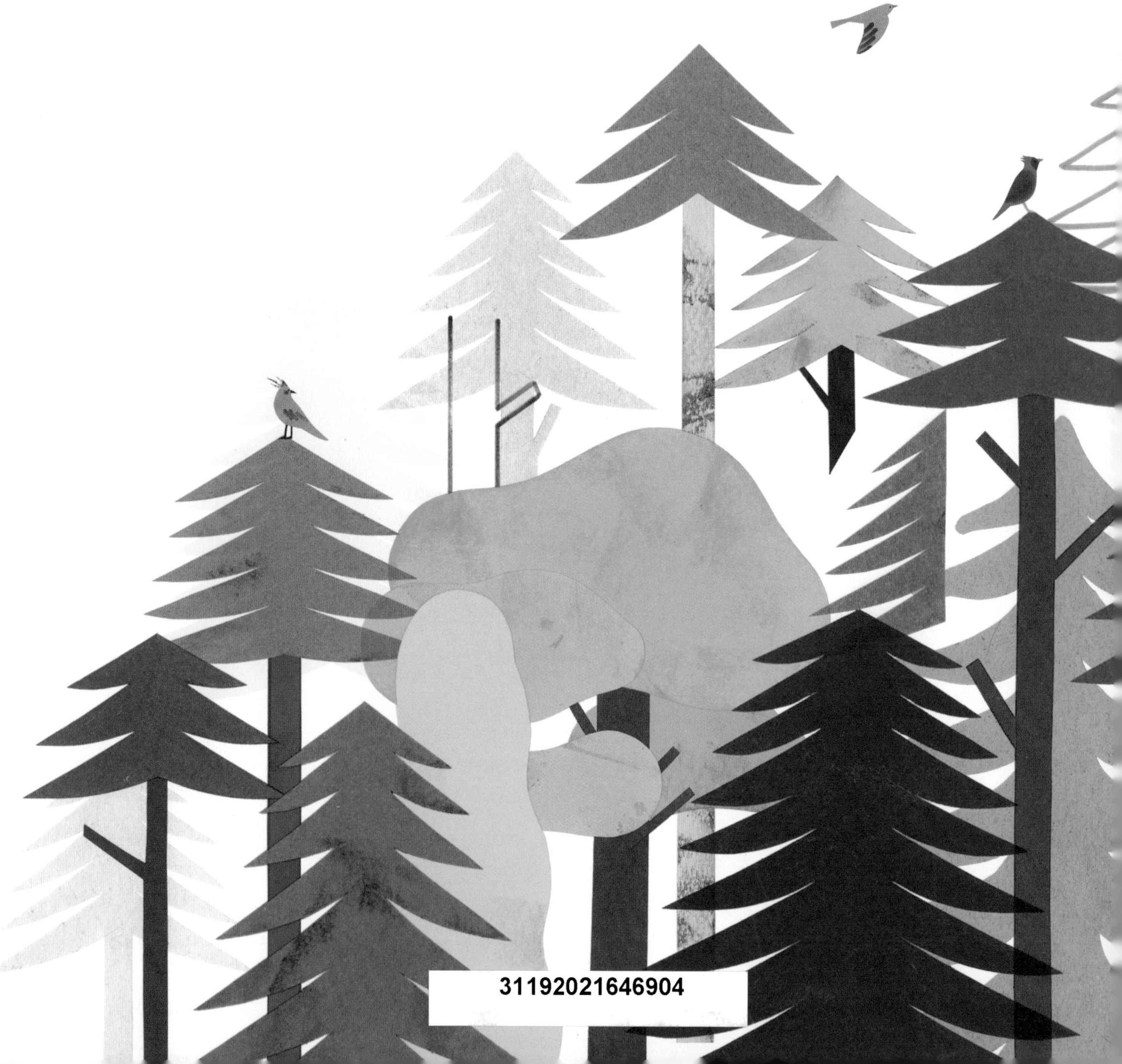